First Pig

Second Pig

Third Pig

HUFF &

Claudia Rueda

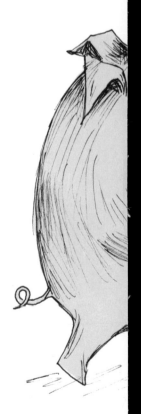

& PUFF

Abrams Appleseed

New York

First pig building a house.

First pig inside the house.

One wolf huffing and puffing.

First pig is not happy.

Second pig building a house.

Second pig inside the house.

One wolf huffing and puffing.

Second pig is not happy.

Third pig building a house.

Third pig inside the house.

One wolf huffing and puffing.

One wolf huffing and puffing,
AGAIN.

(REALLY hard)

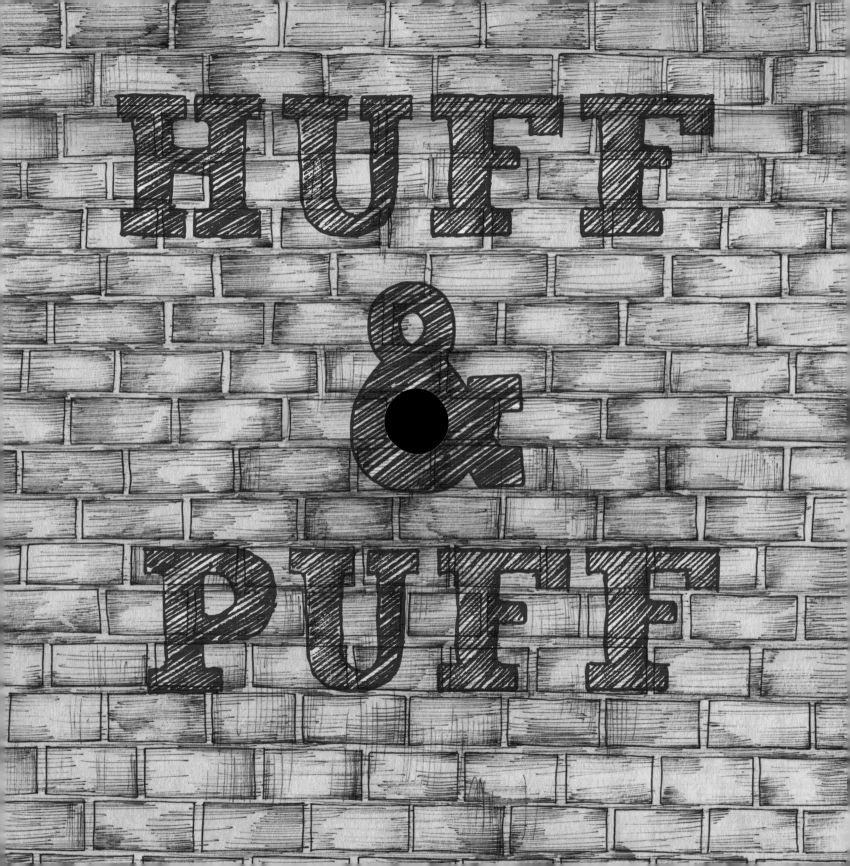

SURPRISE!

One wolf huffed and puffed
and blew the candles out.

Three pigs and one wolf
are happy.